N

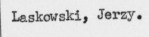

MASTER OF THE ROYAL CATS

MASTER OF

ILLUSTRATED BY JANINA DOMANSKA

THE SEABURY PRESS, NEW YORK

THE ROYAL CATS

BY JERZY LASKOWSKI

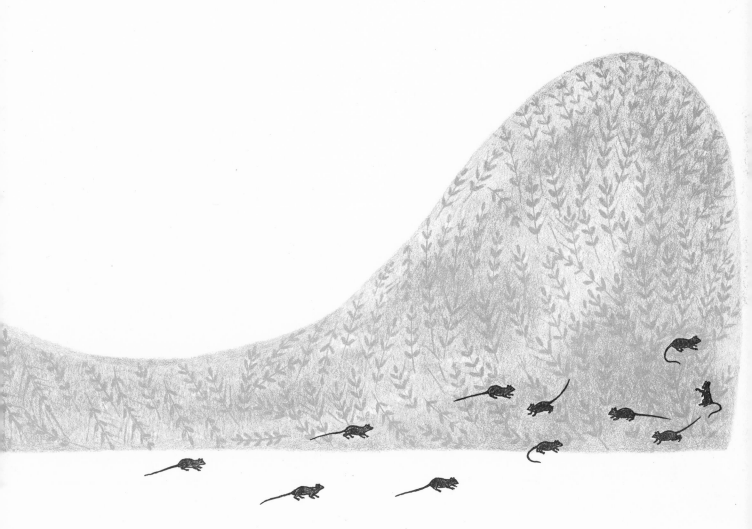

MASTER OF THE ROYAL CATS

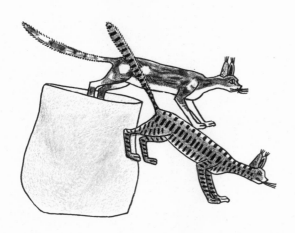

Thousands of years ago in Egypt, when dogs were tame and cats were wild, there was a Pharaoh who lived in a great palace near the pyramids where his ancestors were buried. He was very rich and powerful.

Pharaoh's wealth was his grain. The grain was more precious than gold, and to keep the rats away from the heaps of barley and wheat, Pharaoh had three dogs to guard it night and day. Every evening he would come to look at his grain, and to take a walk in the desert with one of his dogs.

The dogs loved their master, but they were not fond of chasing rats. Except for the evening walks, they thought their lives were very dull.

One bright summer morning when there were no rats in sight, one of the dogs said, "It is a fine day for hunting rabbits."

"But if we leave our posts — " said the second dog.

"Wouldn't we get a beating?" asked the third.

"Nonsense," said the first dog. "Pharaoh loves us too much to beat us. Besides, I think we have frightened away the rats forever."

Off he ran, and began digging at a rabbit hole.

The other dogs watched, and soon their tails began to wag, and off they ran to find rabbit holes of their own.

That night when Pharaoh came, the dogs were missing and the rats were having a feast.

Naturally, Pharaoh was very upset. "The dogs must be found!" he commanded. "And a hundred gold pieces to the finder!"

Three boys set out together to look for the dogs. They were Sati and Bata and Anpu. Anpu was the smallest and the youngest; he was always being teased by the other two.

All day long the boys searched, but they found no trace of the dogs, not even a paw print.

At nightfall they came upon an empty house. There was food on the table and they ate it.

Then Sati and Bata said to Anpu, "We're going to sleep. You must stay up and keep guard." Anpu was tired himself, but there was nothing he could do except obey.

He was nodding with sleep when a big crocodile came in. Anpu jumped up and grabbed the crocodile by the tail.

"Don't be frightened," said the crocodile. "Let me spend the night and I will be your friend. I'm over a hundred years old and I'm sacred. All crocodiles in Egypt are sacred. You know that."

"But crocodiles eat boys," cried Anpu.

"Well, I don't," said the crocodile. "There's no use hanging onto my tail. You see, I could lift you up and throw you over my shoulder. Like this."

The crocodile lifted his tail ever so gently and raised Anpu off his feet.

"Yes, I can see that," said Anpu.

"You're a brave boy and I like you," said the crocodile. "Go to sleep and I'll keep watch. And in the morning I'll tell you where to find Pharaoh's dogs."

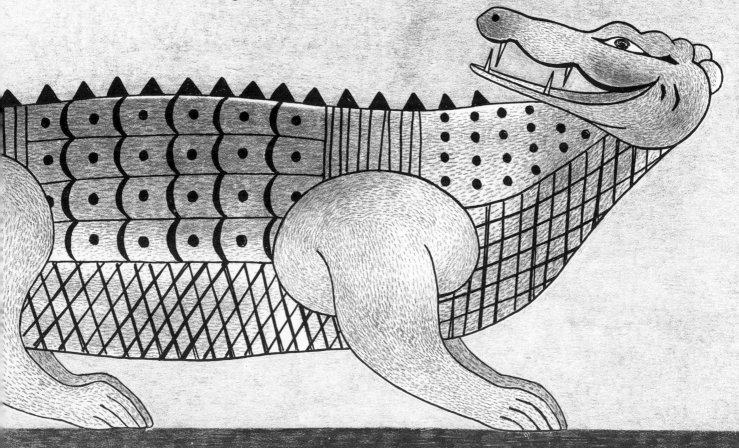

And in the morning that is just what the crocodile did. To all three of the boys he said, "Walk due north for half a day, then due west until sundown." Sati and Bata ran off without a word.

"Just as I thought; they have no manners at all," said the crocodile.

To Anpu he said, "Follow them, but don't worry about the dogs. Keep your eyes open for something much better."

At sundown, sure enough, there were the dogs, very busy watching rabbit holes. Sati and Bata captured them with shouts of joy.

Anpu remembered what the crocodile had said, and he looked all around,
and what did he see but —
two wild and hungry cats, who had just found a rat!
Anpu caught the cats and put them into his sack.

When Sati and Bata saw what Anpu had done with the cats, they laughed and called him names and threw rocks at him, until he ran away and hid.

"Good riddance," said Sati and Bata. They found a boat at the bank of the Nile river and left with the dogs for the journey home.

Anpu was very unhappy. He had no boat, and he didn't know the way home. At that moment his friend the crocodile appeared.

"So you did find something better," said the crocodile. "Now let's be on our way."

Up the Nile river swam the big crocodile, with Anpu on his back holding tight to the sack full of cats. In no time at all they caught up with the boys and the dogs in the boat.

"Jump on my back," said the crocodile to the dogs. And he upset the boat with a mighty flip of his tail. "The boys can swim home."

When Anpu and the dogs and the cats arrived at the royal palace,
they found Pharaoh in a terrible state of nerves.

His soldiers were trying to guard the grain, but the rats were much too quick for them and were dashing around and eating their fill.

Pharaoh was overjoyed to see his dogs back again. "Now we'll have no more rats," he cried. "Good dogs! Catch those rats!"

But the three dogs just sat. Pharaoh turned on Anpu in a fury and said, "Boy, you have bewitched my beautiful dogs. Unbewitch them, or I will chop off your head."

Anpu bowed low and said, "Mighty Pharaoh, your dogs are not bewitched. Now that they have hunted rabbits, they have no taste for rats. But I have brought you something better. Here are two animals who are most interested in rats. I offer them to you with the compliments of the sacred crocodile."

Out of the sack jumped the wild and hungry cats. Before Pharaoh could stroke his beard, all the rats had vanished.

"What marvelous animals!" said Pharaoh. "In the future they will guard my grain.

"The reward is yours," he said to Anpu, "and a title, too. You shall be known as Master of the Royal Cats."

From that day on, the dogs went rabbit hunting whenever they pleased.

And the cats never tired of watching over Pharaoh's grain and keeping the rats away.